Papa's Gift

An Inspirational Story of Love and Loss

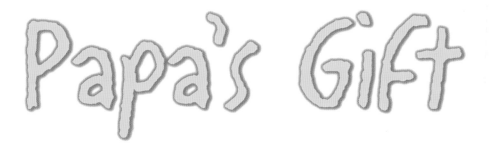

Written by KATHLEEN LONG BOSTROM

Illustrated by GUY PORFIRIO

Zonder**kidz**

On the very day he turned sixty-three, Clarence MacKenzie received the best birthday present in the world. His first grandchild, Clara, was born.

"From now on I shall be called Papa Clarence," he told his family. And that was that.

Not only did Clara and Papa Clarence share the same birthday; they had the same name. Well, almost. They even looked alike.

"But someday you'll have hair," Papa said with a grin, "and I never will have hair again."

He was right.

Papa Clarence had his own room in the house where Clara lived with her mother and father. In the corner, by the window, sat a large, worn rocking chair. "I used to rock your mama in this chair," he said to Clara as he held her in his lap and told her stories. She loved to hear his stories.

"When I was a little boy," he always began, "I hid an icicle under my pillow one night so I could eat it after everyone else went to sleep."

"And did you eat it?" Clara asked him.

"No," Papa Clarence answered. "But I woke up with a big puddle under my pillow!" Then they rocked and laughed as the chair sang, "Creak-crick, creak-crick."

These two best friends did everything together. Every morning they sat together at the kitchen table and ate their cereal. "One spoon of sugar for me, and two for you," Papa Clarence said, winking and dumping an extra spoonful of sugar on Clara's cereal.

Every afternoon they took naps. Clara didn't always sleep, but she could tell by the snores coming from Papa Clarence's room as she tiptoed past that he did.

Every night before bedtime Papa Clarence rocked Clara in the large, worn rocker and told her Bible stories. "When I was a little boy," he began, "I liked to pretend that I was one of the animals on the ark with Noah."

"What animal did you pretend to be?" asked Clara.

"A hoofalopalus!" Papa answered. Then they rocked and laughed as the chair sang, "Creak-crick, creak-crick."

After stories Papa Clarence and Clara knelt by the side of her bed and said their prayers.

Papa Clarence always ended his prayer with, "Thank you, God, for Clara." Clara always ended her prayer with, "Thank you, God, for Papa Clarence." Then together they said, "Amen."

Every week Papa Clarence and Clara sat together in church. Clara's mother and father came, too, but Clara insisted on sitting next to Papa Clarence. He helped Clara follow the words in the hymnbook. He held her hand when they prayed. And he kept a pocket full of red-and-white peppermints that he would slip to Clara, one by one, when nobody was watching.

Papa Clarence loved the snow. And for no other reason than that, Clara loved the snow, too. When the first snow fell, silent and soft, Clara and Papa Clarence held hands and gazed out the window at the snowflakes as they swirled and twirled in the winter air. Each year Papa Clarence taught Clara something new about the snow.

"Anybody can catch snowflakes on their tongue," Papa Clarence told Clara. "But not everyone knows how to make a snowflake sandwich." He took four slices of bread and sprinkled them with lots of sugar. They dressed in their boots and coats and gloves and hurried outside into the snow.

"Like this, Clara," Papa Clarence said, handing her two slices of sugared bread. He held his slices of bread with both hands while the snowflakes piled high. Suddenly Papa clapped his two slices of bread shut. Clara did the same. "The secret is in catching just the perfect snowflakes," Papa Clarence said as he bit into his sandwich.

Clara took a bite of hers. "Needs a bit more sugar," she said.

Another time Papa Clarence and Clara held their breath and fell backward onto the fresh, white blanket of snow. "Wave your arms but not your legs," he said. Papa helped Clara to her feet, and they looked at the strange shapes in the snow.

"Anybody can make a snow angel," Papa Clarence told Clara. "But not everyone knows how to make a snow chicken." He took off one of his gloves and laid it at the top of the snow print he had made. Clara did the same. The glove looked like a chicken's comb. Then Papa pulled two carrots out of his pocket and showed Clara where to place them to look like chickens' beaks.

"The secret is in choosing just the right glove and carrot," Papa said, smiling proudly at his snow chicken.

Clara bent down and rolled several small snowballs. "Snow eggs," she said, placing them by her snow chicken.

Papa laughed. "Good, Clara, good!"

"Cock-a-doodle-do!" Papa Clarence crowed, flapping his arms like wings. Papa and Clara strutted in the snow around their snow chickens, crowing and laughing until their sides hurt.

Papa rocked Clara in the large, worn rocker and told her stories.

"When I was a little boy," he began, "I jumped off the barn roof with an umbrella to see if I could fly."

"And could you?" Clara asked him.

"No," he answered. "But I did a nice dive into the haystack!" And they rocked and they laughed, and the chair sang, "Creak-crick, creak-crick."

One year on their birthday Clara gave her grandfather a striped knit hat. "To keep your head warm when the snows come," she told him.

Papa Clarence grinned and rubbed his bald head. Then he put on the hat and pulled it down until his whole face was covered. "How do I look, Clara?" he asked in a muffled voice.

"Oh, Papa," she said, laughing. "You are so silly!"

Papa Clarence pulled the hat up just enough so he could see and handed Clara a box wrapped with green foil and a red velvet bow. Carefully she unwrapped the box.

Tucked inside Clara found a beautiful glass snow globe. She held it up and saw a little church with a tiny steeple and colored-glass windows. Bits of snow glittered in the light. When she shook the globe, the snow swirled and twirled around the little church.

I t's perfect!" Clara squealed with delight.

"Look very closely," Papa Clarence said. "Who do you see inside the church?"

Clara looked carefully. "I can't see in the windows," she said.

"You'll have to close your eyes to see," Papa said and winked.

"Funny Papa! I can't see with my eyes closed!" Clara said, laughing.

Papa Clarence took the snow globe and held it up to the light. "I taught you how to make a snowflake sandwich. I taught you how to make a snow chicken. These are things that you can see with your eyes. But there are some things you can only see with your heart. Someday you will know."

Clara kept the snow globe on a table next to her bed. She stared at the little church with the tiny steeple and the colored windows and tried to guess who was inside. Every night she shook the globe and watched the flakes swirl and twirl as she drifted to sleep.

That winter, when the first snow fell, silent and soft, Papa Clarence put on his new striped hat. Papa Clarence and Clara pulled on their boots and coats and gloves and hurried outside.

The two best friends ate snowflake sandwiches and made a whole row of snow chickens. They strutted and crowed and flapped their arms like wings. "Keep trying, Papa Clarence!" Clara said. "Maybe someday you'll fly!"

Then one day Papa Clarence woke up with a fever. His breathing sounded wheezy and loud. Clara brought him cold water and held the cup while he sipped through a straw. At night she knelt by her bed and prayed that Papa would get well.

But Papa Clarence did not get well. As each day passed, he grew sicker and sicker. One night the ambulance came and took him to the hospital.

Clara could not sleep that night. She lay in bed and stared at the snow globe. She prayed an extra prayer. "Please, God," she whispered. "Let my Papa be okay." But the next day Papa Clarence died.

When Clara's mother and father told her what had happened, she ran to her room and slammed the door. She threw herself on her bed, curled up under her blanket, and cried and cried. Through her tears she saw the snow globe on the table by her bed. "Papa Clarence was wrong!" she said, sobbing. "There is nobody in the church. The church is empty! God did not answer my prayer. God let Papa die." She took the snow globe and stuffed it under her bed and went to sleep without saying her prayers.

Clara would not be comforted. She would not allow her father to put an extra spoonful of sugar on her cereal. She refused to take a nap, even when her mother lay down on the bed beside her. She would not let anyone rock her in the large, worn rocker, which did not sing anymore.

Clara went to church and sat between her mother and father, but she would not take the red-and-white peppermints they slipped to her when nobody was looking. When everyone else in the church bowed their heads to pray, Clara sat on her hands and stared straight ahead.

One morning Clara woke to find the snow falling, silent and soft. Clara watched the snow through her bedroom window and cried. "I miss you so much, Papa Clarence," she whispered in the quiet.

She reached under her pillow and pulled out Papa Clarence's knit hat, which she had hidden after he died. She rubbed its softness against her cheek and pulled it on her head. Then Clara took the snow globe from under her bed. She tiptoed down the hall to Papa Clarence's empty room. Slowly she opened the door and stepped inside.

In the corner, by the window, sat the large, worn rocking chair. It seemed like such a long time since she had listened to Papa tell his stories.

Still holding the snow globe, Clara climbed into the rocking chair. She shook the globe and watched the snowflakes swirl and twirl around the little church.

She rocked back and forth, back and forth. "Creak-crick, creak-crick," the chair began to sing. Clara remembered Papa Clarence's stories, about the time he slept with an icicle underneath his pillow and how he jumped off the barn roof with an umbrella to see if he could fly. She tried to imagine what a hoofalopalus might look like.

She looked at the snow globe. Bits of snow glittered in the light. She could almost feel the cold flakes kiss her cheek.

Clara remembered when Papa Clarence taught her how to make snowflake sandwiches. She watched the flakes in the globe swirl and twirl and thought about the snow chickens with the carrot beaks that they made each year.

She stared hard at the little church with the tiny steeple, covered with sparkling snow. Then Clara closed her eyes.

She remembered how it felt to sit next to Papa Clarence in church and how he helped her follow the words in the hymnbook. She remembered how warm Papa's hand felt when they prayed, how sweet the red-and-white peppermints tasted that he slipped to her, one by one, when nobody was watching.

"You were right, Papa Clarence," she said, smiling through her tears. "The church is not empty. I can't see you with my eyes anymore. But I can see you with my heart."

She slid from the rocker and gently placed the snow globe on the seat. She ran from Papa's room, leaving the door open behind her.

Clara took four slices of bread from the kitchen and sprinkled them with sugar. Then she grabbed two large carrots from the refrigerator and stuffed them in her pockets. She pulled on her boots and her coat and her gloves and hurried outside.

Clara caught snowflakes on the bread and ate both sandwiches. She fell backward into the snow and made a snow chicken. Next to it she made another snow chicken for Papa Clarence. She took off her gloves and put one on the head of each snow chicken and carefully added the carrot beaks.

Bits of snow glittered in the light, and the flakes swirled and twirled around her. "Anybody can have a grandpa," Clara whispered. "But not everyone has a grandpa like my Papa Clarence."

That night Clara set the snow globe on the table next to her bed. Then she knelt to say her prayers for the first time since Papa Clarence died.

"Thank you, God, for all the things I can see with my eyes," she began her prayer. "Like snowflake sandwiches and snow chickens and red-and-white peppermints. And thank you, God, for all the things I can see with my heart. Like Papa Clarence. And you. Amen."

Clara climbed into bed and snuggled under the covers. Her mother and father came and tucked her in. "Tomorrow morning," she said, "I'd like an extra spoonful of sugar on my cereal. And don't forget the peppermints for church." After Clara's mother and father left her room, she reached under her pillow and felt the icicle she had placed there.

As sleep fell, silent and soft, upon her, Clara dreamed about Papa Clarence jumping off a barn roof with an umbrella to see if he could fly.

He did.

To my grandmother, Edith May Johnson, with love.

And in memory of my mother, Mary, whose mother's name was Clara;
and in memory of my husband's grandmother, Mary, whose husband's name was Clarence.

— *K.L.B.*

To my lovely wife Gabriela and our two wonderful children David and Katherine.

Special thanks to Molly.

— *G.P.*

Zonderkidz

The children's group of Zondervan

www.zonderkidz.com

Papa's Gift
ISBN: 0-310-70923-7
Copyright © 2002 by Kathleen Long Bostrom
Illustrations copyright © 2002 by Guy Porfirio

Requests for information should be addressed to:
Zonderkidz, Grand Rapids, Michigan 49530

Editor: Gwen Ellis
Art Direction and Design: Jody Langley

Printed in China
04 05 06 07/HK/4 3 2 1